NEVER BORED ON THE FARM

by Alex Vern

illustrated by Marion Eldridge

Harcourt

Orlando   Boston   Dallas   Chicago   San Diego

Visit *The Learning Site!*

www.harcourtschool.com

It's never boring on my family's farm.
You might suppose that I wake up very
early every morning. You would be right!

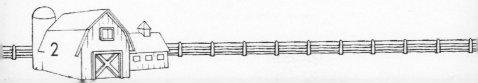

Every day I get up *before* the sun
rises. If I waited for the sun to rise, I'd
never get my chores done.

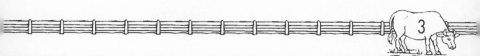

First I go to milk our three cows. My
dad told me the best way to milk a cow.
He told me that if I crouched down
and ducked my head, I could see what
I'm doing. That made sense!

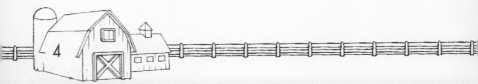

After I milk the cows, I check out
the chicken coop.

Our hens' eggs are delicious. We eat some and sell the rest at our farm stand.

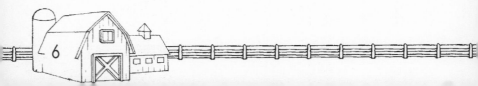

Then I look in on the pigs. They are always loud. Sometimes they fight over their food.

By this time I'm really hungry.
Breakfast includes some of the eggs
that the hens just laid!

If it's a school day, my sister and I
run to catch the school bus.

If it's not a school day, I go into the
garden to see what needs to be done.
The vegetables and fruits might need
to be watered.

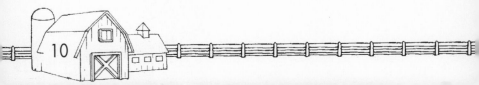

The soil might need to be weeded. Some vegetables or fruits might be ready for picking.

My dad spends a lot of time out in the fields. He might be plowing with the tractor to plant soybeans or wheat.

Sometimes I help out at our farm stand. We sell our extra fruits and vegetables as well as fresh eggs.

By the time I've eaten dinner and done my homework, I'm tired. Sometimes I'm ready for bed before the sun goes down.

It's easy to fall asleep when you're really tired. A long day of school and chores wears me out!

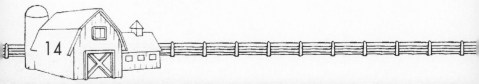

Before I know it, it's time to get up.
The cows are waiting for me.

As you can see, I am never bored on the farm!

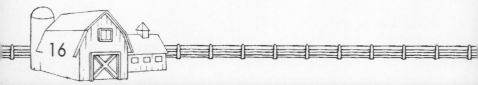